ADAM HANCHER

The Little Pioneer

One young girl's story . . .

Frances Lincoln
Children's Books

In the fall of 1849, Papa passed on.
He left to us a new homestead, but it was so far away.

"A new life!" declared Ma as we piled our belongings
into the rickety wooden wagon.

Spring had arrived, and we were
moving to California.

We gathered at
the edge of Independence,
four families all moving West.

We knew little about the trip across the Plains, but everyone had
great faith in the seasoned captain, a gruff old mountain
man by the name of Mr. Reed.

Packed, mounted, and yoked, we bid
our old life farewell.

"Westward ho!" boomed Mr. Reed, setting me to fright!

It was a fearful time in those early days,

and no doubt we all thought the same . . .

That our journey was to be terribly long.

My brothers soon
took to life on the prairie.
I did not.

My chores were dull and tiresome,
and I would avoid the uncultivated
Mr. Reed at all costs.

"He's a wild man!" I said to Ma.

"It helps to know wild folks when in a wild place," Ma said
as we prepared to cross the mighty Platte River.

Ma was never wrong.

That river was treacherous, swift, and swollen!

Before I knew it, the river tore me from our wagon.

Flopping and flailing, I was carried downstream,

sure I would be drowned.

But Mr. Reed, bold as ever,

plucked me from the perilous waters,

choking, soaked, and altogether shaken up.

"Thank the Lord for Mr. Reed!" Ma exclaimed.

"You owe that man an apology."

Oh, how ignorant I had been!

"Ma . . . How can I make amends?" I asked.

"You should ask Mr. Reed," she replied.

So I did.

"How can I repay you, sir?" I asked.

Mr. Reed hooted, "We'll start with this here fire—
that'll dry you out!"

With fire came toasted bread, biscuits, and buffalo stew.

Our company felt like family as we all sang to the stars.

Mr. Reed was quite at home out in the wilderness, but I had much to learn.
Our old lives seemed so distant, and California felt no closer.

For months, we labored on along that dusty emigrant trail.

The good times passed and hardship followed.

Our wagons broke, the oxen tired,

and sickness struck us down.

Weary and footsore, we stopped to rest.

While the burdens we could no longer bear were unloaded,

I sought a shady spot for a moment's peace.

Never had I slept so soundly than

when under that great tree.

Trouble was, when I awoke . . .

I was all alone.

"Maaa!" I yelled with all
my might, but there was no reply.
"Mr. Reed?" I called
to no avail.

Wagon tracks scarred
the rocky landscape,
but which should I follow?
Clueless, I stumbled
deeper into the hills.

As night fell,
winter's icy fingers
slid through the trees.
Cold and alone, my
thoughts went to Mr. Reed.
He would not despair.
He would get to work,
set up camp, and . . .

"We'll start with a fire!"
That was it.
Gathering leaves, bark,
and branches, I remembered
what I had been taught.

With flint and stone, I lit my tinder.
Sparks grew to embers, embers set
ablaze, and soon enough—

My fire roared!

Oh, how that fire lifted my spirits.
I felt safe in the warmth,
but with the fire shining
bright, I could see creatures
all around me. Mice rustled
underfoot, owls hooted
overhead, and . . . What was
that creeping toward me
out of the shadows?

Ragged and wild, it staggered out of the darkness, fearsomely mad.

But folks must be wild in a wild place—so, cornered and panicked,
I pulled a branch from the fire. "Not now, bear!" I shouted.

"Woooa!" coughed Mr. Reed, appearing through the smoke. "I ain't no bear."

What a relief it was to see that face!

"I didn't think I'd find you, till you went a' lit that fire," he said.

"I've taken quite a liking to the wilderness," I replied.

"A real pioneer!" laughed Mr. Reed.

We woke at daybreak
and raced to the wagons.
The cold mountains
faded behind us.

The dreads and fears fell away from Ma when she saw that I was safe.

Even my brothers put mischief aside to greet me.

In truth, all were in high spirits.

We had arrived in California.

Our company shared its final good-byes, as we bid farewell to life on the trail.

"Westward ho!" I shouted.

Our new lives lay just over the hill…

For us—and for Mr. Reed, too.

To Margaret and Gary - A.H.

Little Pioneer © Frances Lincoln 2016
Text and illustrations copyright © Adam Hancher 2016
The right of Adam Hancher to be identified as the author and illustrator of this work has been asserted by him
in accordance with the Copyright, Designs and Patents Act, 1988 (United Kingdom).

First published in Great Britain in 2016 by Frances Lincoln Children's Books, 74-77 White Lion Street, London N1 9PF
QuartoKnows.com
Visit our blogs at QuartoKnows.com

A catalogue record for this book is available from the British Library.

ISBN 978-1-84780-798-4

Illustrated digitally
Designed by Mike Jolley. Edited by Jenny Broom. Production by Jenny Cundill.

Printed in China
1 3 5 7 9 8 6 4 2